ALFIE

Based on *The Railway Series* by the Rev. W. Awdry

Illustrations by
Robin Davies and Jerry Smith

EGMONT

EGMONT

We bring stories to life

First published in Great Britain in 2007
by Egmont UK Limited
239 Kensington High Street, London W8 6SA
All Rights Reserved

HiT entertainment

ISBN 978 1 4052 3298 2
3 5 7 9 10 8 6 4
Printed in Italy

This is a story about Alfie the Excavator. Some of The Pack teased him about being small, until he proved that you can be Useful no matter what size you are . . .

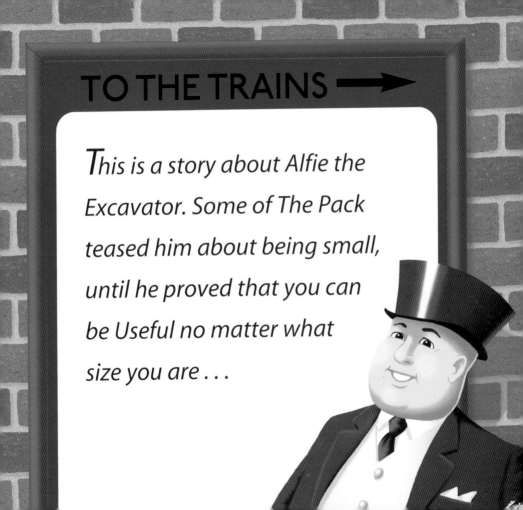

It was a beautiful day on the Island of Sodor. Thomas had brought his friend, Alfie the Excavator, to a demolition site where The Pack were working.

"Hello, Thomas!" rattled Jack the Digger.

"Hello, Jack!" puffed Thomas. "I've brought Alfie to help you on the site."

"I love demolition!" said Alfie. "It's when we get to knock buildings down!"

Thomas couldn't understand why the machines would enjoy that!

"Is demolition fun?" he asked.

"The best fun!" cried Alfie, and he swooped down the ramp.

"Look out, small fry!" boomed Monty the Dump Truck.

"I'm not small fry!" said Alfie, crossly.

Alfie *was* small for an Excavator, but he didn't like being teased about his size.

Alfie was happy when the Foreman sent him to work with Ned the Steam Shovel. He knew that Ned wouldn't try to make him feel small.

But as Alfie pulled up, Ned swung his bucket.

"Watch out!" cried Alfie.

"Sorry, Alfie," said Ned. "I didn't see you. You're smaller than you look!"

This made Alfie feel even smaller.

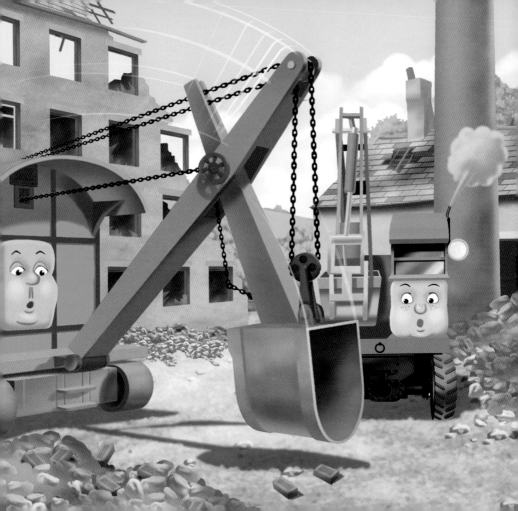

The demolition site was very busy and Alfie was working hard. But some of The Pack were still being mean to him.

"Hurry up, half-pint," teased Monty.

"It's not half-pint," sneered Max. "It's small fry."

Alfie was very upset.

At the tea break, Thomas could see that Alfie was unhappy.

"What's wrong, Alfie?" he asked.

"I don't like being small," complained Alfie.

"As long as you're Useful," said Thomas helpfully, "it doesn't matter what size you are!"

Alfie thought about this for a moment.

"Tea break's over," shouted Kelly, "back to work."

That afternoon, Alfie was determined to be Really Useful.

He was helping Oliver the Big Excavator demolish a building.

Oliver's giant scissor claw grabbed the top of the wall.

"Stop!" cried Alfie. "I can hear something!"

Everyone stopped work, but no one could hear a thing.

"I checked inside and it's empty," said the Foreman.

"Small fry is hearing things," sneered Max.

"I did hear something, I really did," said Alfie.

The Foreman looked inside again and he was surprised to find the building wasn't empty!

"There's a mother cat in here, and she's got kittens!" he said.

"We must rescue them!" said Alfie.

"The building isn't safe," said the Foreman. "I can't send my men in there."

"I'll go!" said Alfie, bravely. "I'm small enough to fit in."

In no time, Alfie wriggled inside. The building creaked and plaster flew.

Alfie held up his scoop for the cat and kittens to jump in.

"Here, kitty, kitty," Alfie coaxed.

But the cat and kittens didn't move.

Suddenly, the upper wall started to crumble.

"Hurry, kitty, kitty," cried Alfie.

But it was too late. The bricks were falling around him.

Alfie would need to act fast!

Quick as a wink, Alfie covered the cat and her kittens with his bucket. He was just in time.

"Miaow," said the cat.

"Miaow, miaow," said the kittens.

"Phew!" said Alfie.

The cat and kittens were safe.

"Well done, Alfie," said Miss Jenny. "And a fine family of kittens it is."

"I couldn't have rescued them if I'd been any bigger," said Alfie.

"You may be small," said Kelly. "But you've got a big heart."

"And a Really Useful bucket!" said Thomas.

Alfie felt very proud. And he never complained about being small again.

The Thomas Story Library is THE definitive collection of stories about Thomas and ALL his friends.

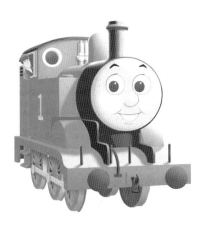

There are now 50 stories
from the Island of Sodor
to collect!

So go on, start your Thomas Story Library NOW!

A Fantastic Offer for Thomas the Tank Engine Fans!

STICK POUND COIN HERE

In every Thomas Story Library book like this one, you will find a special token. Collect 6 Thomas tokens and we will send you a brilliant Thomas poster, and a double-sided bedroom door hanger! Simply tape a £1 coin in the space above, and fill out the form overleaf.

TO BE COMPLETED BY AN ADULT

To apply for this great offer, ask an adult to complete the coupon below and send it with a pound coin and 6 tokens, to:
THOMAS OFFERS, PO BOX 715, HORSHAM RH12 5WG

☐ Please send a Thomas poster and door hanger. I enclose 6 tokens plus a £1 coin. (Price includes P&P)

Fan's name...

Address...

....Postcode...............................

Date of birth...

Name of parent/guardian...

Signature of parent/guardian..

Please allow 28 days for delivery. Offer is only available while stocks last. We reserve the right to change the terms of this offer at any time and we offer a 14 day money back guarantee. This does not affect your statutory rights.

☐ Data Protection Act: If you do not wish to receive other similar offers from us or companies we recommend, please tick this box. Offers apply to UK only.